Duke Hyde

An Original Screenplay

Jesse W. Bolero

First Edition

PAGE PUBLISHING, INC.
New York, NY

First originally published by Page Publishing, Inc. 2019

ISBN 978-1-64462-925-3 (Paperback)
ISBN 978-1-64462-927-7 (Digital)

Printed in the United States of America

CASTS

Duke Hyde… Black
Doris… Black
Dan… Black
Fran… White
Kate… White
Mother… Black
May… Black
Ruth… White
Sandy… White
Larry… White
John… White
Doctor… Black
The supremes… Black
Old woman… Puerto Rican
Sister… Puerto Rican

(*Lights up on.*)

This is a black story…

New York City—Sin City, 1969, where children die very young from Dope. The big *H* is hell—and who cares?

New York City—where getting dope is as easy and free as the wind.

(*Music.*)

(*The first scene takes place in Duke Hyde's five-room apartment [no. 16] at 1375 Central Park, West in New York City. It is on the first floor.*)

Duke is thirty years old, a tall, good-looking black man who has everything a man could want. He is a drug addict and a drinker—a gin drinker.

His living room resembles a nightclub, with its bar, pictures of theatrical entertainers, and many books of black greats.

Duke is a very intelligent man who graduated from Morehouse College, majoring in health education, when he was twenty years old.

(*The lights are up on Duke. He is in bed reading a Black Panther newspaper. The television set is on, soft music playing.*)

(*A cat and a dog are scampering about the room—his pets.*)

(*Duke puts newspaper down and picks up a JET news book. After a moment, he puts the book down, gives himself a shot of Heroin. Shortly after, he is turned into a violent "wolf" man. He kills the cat then pulls its head off. He tries to get the dog who has run under the bed to hide, almost overturning the bed to get at the dog. The dog escapes and hides in the apartment.*)

(*Duke goes to an open window and looks outside, wildly. Two girls passing see his face and run up the street screaming.*)

(*Lights on to them as they run.*)

(*Lights return to Duke, as he gets on to the bed where he passes out. Lights slowly fade out…*)

(*The next day.*)

(*Lights fade in on Duke, and the headless cat on the bed. The bed is spattered with the cat's blood, its head on the floor.*)

(*The doorbell rings, then rings again.*)

(*Duke jumps to his feet, looks around, sees the cat's body and head. He picks these up, rushes to the kitchen looking for a hiding place. He stuffs both the body and head in the icebox, then returns to bedroom and covers the blood-spattered bed.*)

(*The doorbell rings again.*)

DUKE, *calling loudly*.

(*The dog runs to the door, barking.*)

(*The doorbell rings again, as Duke goes to door.*)

DAN'S VOICE, *in hall*. It's me—Dan.

(*Lights go to Dan, as Duke opens the door. The dog runs out.*)

DUKE, *calling to dog*. Come back here. (*He runs down the hall stairs after the dog, leaving Dan standing at open door.*)

(*Lights fade to Duke running after the dog.*)

DAN, *as Duke returns without his dog*. Hi, you doing, man? What's wrong with that dog, Duke?

DUKE, *entering apartment with Dan*. That dumb dog—let him go. He eats too much, anyway like a nigger.

DAN. Man, you look like hell…

DUKE, *interrupting*. I do, do I?

DAN. Are you cool?

DUKE, *changing subject*. Me? Sure. How's your old lady?

DAN. My mother? (*He smiles.*) Oh, she's over on Forty-Ninth Street and Seventh Avenue trying to make rent money.

DUKE, *going to bar and pouring a drink*. I had a crazy nightmare, Dan… (*He thinks.*) Most strange. (*He goes back to bed and sits, holding his head.*)

DAN, *repeating*. You look like hell. Did you take any—

DUKE, *interrupting*. Any what? No… I was born crazy. Dan, I'm a "wolf" man!

DAN, *laughing*. Wolf man? Wolf.

DUKE, *jumping from bed*. You don't have the mind to understand me. You won't believe me. (*Quite upset.*) Why don't you go… Get out of my life.

DAN. Come on now, man.

DUKE, *goes back to bar, pours another drink, then pauses*. This place is honeycombed with secret tunnels, and there's no need to whisper. My grandfather lived here and sometimes I can hear him at this bar, drinking. And the walls are two feet thick on each side.

DAN. So…(*he goes over to Duke*) man, what kind of stuff have you been taking? You talk crazy.

DUKE, *looks at him*. I am crazy… I'm more than one person… I'm two people and you're the first to know.

(*They embrace each other laughing like two hep kids.*)

(*Lights fade slowly out.*)

(*Lights up on Duke, walking along Central Park West in the direction of the subway. He is dressed in a long white robe.*)

(*People passing turn to look at him. He turns as he hears his name being called. He stops and waits for May, a friend.*)

MAY, *calling to Duke.* Hey, Duke… Hey, Duke…

(*Duke and May walk on to subway entrance. Lights are on both of them as they ride a subway train. Everyone stares at them.*)

DUKE, *as they leave subway exit.* I'm going to the bank—I'm broke!

MAY, *smiling.* Is that so? It's hard to believe you're broke—you look so prosperous all the time.

DUKE, *smiles.* And you're riding the subway! Did your private railroad break down?

DUKE. Stop it, my dear, you're too much. (*Irritated.*) And you talk too much and too fast. (*He stops.*) I've got things to do.

MAY. Oh, yes, I was forgetting.

DUKE. Don't forget to stop by the apartment.

(*May crosses the street as Duke enters a bank where he draws out five thousand dollars. As he leaves bank, he sees his friend John, a cab driver, who has stopped. Duke gets in the cab.*)

JOHN. Hop in, Duke.

DUKE. Man, oh man… This is the best time to meet a friend. I've got five thousand dollars on me and I meet my crazy friend. There must be a God… Drive me to my apartment, John.

JOHN, *laughing.* Brother Duke, I'm—glad to see you. Let's get high… I've got some good grass.

DUKE. Take it easy, John, and don't drive so fast. How's your wife and kids?

JOHN. They're all okay, man, and the old lady's head is much better.

DUKE. And your other woman—your girlfriend?

JOHN. Oh, I don't see her any more. (*He looks at Duke.*) She told me you were a cold man for not having her.

DUKE, *holding his head in his hands.* She did? (*Seeing this.*)

JOHN. Duke, are you all right?

DUKE. I'm okay. (*He looks out cab and sees they are at his apartment house.*) Park the cab and come up, John. (*They get out of cab as lights fade out.*)

(*Lights up as they enter Duke's apartment. John goes to the piano and begins playing Beethoven's 5th Symphony. Duke gets a large gold box and places it on the bed.*)

DUKE. There you are, John… Roll, you know I hate to… (*John continues playing the piano until piece is finished.*)

DUKE, *appreciating the music.* That's great, man. Why don't you let the world hear you?

JOHN, *sadly.* Who? Me? Me, John? Yes, I'm going to stop driving a cab, someday. (*He goes to Duke at bed, rolls pot.*)

DUKE, *thinking.* John, do you ever think of death?

JOHN, *happy.* Oh yes, indeed I do. I can't wait to die… But then I believe in the great spirits.

DUKE. Spirits, that's it, spirits—and dreams. That's right. I was only having a nightmare—

JOHN. Sometimes you've got to pray, Duke.

JOHN. Yes…man, this grass is too much.

DUKE. That's right… It's all pure gold.

(*The telephone rings. Duke answers.*)

DUKE. Hello! Yes. Oh, yes, thank you. (*A pause.*) I'll call you if I need you. (*He hangs up.*)

JOHN. I better get out of here.

DUKE. John, I want to see that girl—
JOHN. What girl?
DUKE. You know, your girlfriend.
JOHN. Oh, you mean Kate.
DUKE, *looking very happy*. Yes, Kate.
JOHN. Man, will she be surprised.
DUKE. I'll bet she will.
JOHN. She's listed in the phone book—Kate Goldberg, in Forest Hills… I'll see you, Duke.

(*He leaves apartment.*)

(*Duke goes to kitchen and to ice box. He removes the dead cat and puts both cat and its head in a shopping bag and then goes to an open window and drops the bag out the window. He returns to the Bar and gets a drink. Then he shoots some LSD in his arm. He goes into the bedroom, looks in the wall mirror, and he changes into the "wolf" man. The telephone rings and he answers it.*)
DUKE, *trying to talk but only animal sounds come out*. Ar-ar-ha-ha-ar-ar-ar-ar-ha. (*He hangs up*.)

(*Duke goes to the mirror and looks at himself again. He smashes the mirror into pieces and then goes round and round the room. He passes out as lights fade out.*)

(*Lights up. Next morning, the cleaning woman is sweeping up the broken glass from the mirror. He enters the room.*)
CLEANING WOMAN. Mr. Hyde, are you all right?
DUKE, *dully*. Yes… Why does everyone ask me if I'm all right? Do I look sick?
CLEANING WOMAN, *gravely*. Yes, you do. You look very sick. And all this broken glass—what happened?
DUKE, *quietly*. Oh that… Dan and I were kidding around and—(*a pause*)—yes, that's it. We were kidding around, and we broke the mirror. Ban and I did it. (*He goes out of the room to the bar,*

pours a drink, then goes to phone book and looks up a number and calls Kate. Into phone:) Hello, Kate? This is Duke…

(*The lights go on Kate, in her bathroom, preparing to bathe. An extension cord from her bedroom enables her to talk on phone.*)

KATE, *surprised.* Oh, Hi, Duke, I can't believe this is you—Duke Hyde. It's good to hear you, I was just getting into the tub.

(*The lights break on Duke, drinking.*)

DUKE. I was just thinking about you. I have missed you.
KATE. Come, now… How can you miss anyone or anything…
DUKE, *a pause.* My secret—I missed you.
KATE. Are you sure you're all right?
DUKE. Yes… How about a date?
KATE. For when? Should I rush?
DUKE. Not so fast—but rush! How about going to the Royal Box tonight? The supremes are there. Dinner and all? How about it? You can't say "No."
KATE, *laughs.* If you put it like that, I can't say no. Yes, Duke, I'll do whatever you say.
DUKE. I'll be there soon.
KATE. What do you call soon? I'm just getting into the tub.
DUKE. I'll be there about ten thirty.
KATE. Good. See you soon, honey. (*She hangs up.*)

Lights up on Duke, holding the phone on the word honey. Duke goes to the piano and plays the tune "Satin Doll" and he sees his hand start changing to a "wolf's" hand. He gets up, runs to the bar, talking to himself.

DUKE, *to himself.* I've got to tell Mama…

(*As he picks up the phone, the lights are on the "wolf" hand, and it changes, back to a human hand.*)

DUKE, *to himself, very disturbed.* My no-good father was a crazy man... He had to be... (*Lights fade out quickly.*)

(*Lights up on Duke in his white Rolls Royce, later that evening. Larry and he are in the car. Duke is talking.*)

DUKE. Larry, I'm going to the West Coast. Would you rather come to Duke? (*continuing*) California or stay here in New York? It's a good time to go now. (*He pauses.*) But then it's nice all the time in California.

LARRY. I think I'd better stay here. My old lady's been thinking about trading me in for a black man...

DUKE, *laughing heartily.* (*Lights fade*)—You better decide. Black folks are getting to be something else.

(*Lights out.*)

(*Larry end Duke get out of car. Duke goes to an apartment house, rings doorbell.*)

KATE, *opening the door*, (*happily*). Mr. Hyde... You look great, Duke. (*They kiss.*)

DUKE. Think so?

(*Lights up on them. Kate and Duke walk to car and enter. Larry who has been waiting, closes door after them.*)

KATE, *holding cigarette.* It's like old times being out with you again, Duke.

(*Duke smiles. The car takes off quickly.*)

(*Lights out.*)

(*Lights up at the Americana Hotel. The doorman opens car door. Duke and Kate go into the hotel and to the Royal Box. A headwaiter takes them to their table right up front.*)

(*Lights go to Richard Pryor on stage where he is telling some jokes, then lights go to Duke and Kate.*)

DUKE, *about to give order to waiter.* What will you have to drink? I'm drinking gin.

KATE. Gin? That's a sex drink.

DUKE. It's good… I recommend it.

KATE, *happily.* I'll have whatever you have.

(*Lights go back on Richard Pryor onstage.*)

RICHARD, *continues to audience.* And, folks, out there among you, I can see any number of hit recording stars. (*Lights pan to the audience and stop at some of the stars present.*) Sammy Davis, Gladys Knight, Eddie Kendix, and others.

(*Lights back to Richard Pryor on stage.*)

RICHARD. Thank you. Now, don't any of you move, because the great supremes are here to sing for y'all.

(*He exits from stage and lights fade down to a blue light.*)

(*Voice.*)

And now the Royal Box presents the world great supremes. They come on stage and begin their act. (*Lights on them.*)

(*Lights go to Duke.*)

DUKE, *to Kate.* That Jean is good.

KATE. She sings better than Diane, I think.

Duke looks at one of his hands as it begins to resemble a "wolf hand." He jumps up and runs out of the Supper Club, leaving Kate alone at table. He goes to the lobby and once more looks at his hand which has now turned back into a human hand.

(*Lights are back on the supremes. They do their next act.*)

MARY. Hello, my name is Mary... Like in "Mary had a little Lamb..." (*The audience applauds.*)

CINDY. And my name is Cindy Birdsong. Like in birds sing. (*The audience applauds.*)

JEAN. And me... I used to be the new one, but that didn't last long. My name is Jean Terrell. Ernie Terrell's sister, not Diane Ross. (*The audience applauds.*)

(*The supremes sing "Nathan Jones"...*)

(*Lights on Duke, walking back to his table. He sits down.*)

KATE. Duke Hyde, how could you go to John when the supremes are here to entertain you.

DUKE, *angrily.* I had to go... I go whenever I have to. Even if Dr. King were here, I'd still go...

KATE, *lightly.* Okay, darling.

DUKE, *calm down.* Am I your darling?

KATE. If you want to be. (*She hesitates.*) But please, let's not fight.

DUKE, *simply.* We won't, darling.

(*Lights go to the supremes.*)

(*The headwaiter brings a telephone to Duke's table.*)

(*Lights on Duke.*)

HEADWAITER. Mr. Hyde, a call for you...

Duke, *into phone*. Yes, Larry. That dumb dog… We're drinking now. The show will be over in about fifteen minutes. (*A pause.*) Okay, then go and get him, Larry. (*To Kate.*) They found my dog. (*He hangs up.*)
Kate. Good. Duke… (*She hesitates.*) You get whatever you want…
Duke, *his eyes smiling*. Are you saying that I've got you?
Kate. Mr. Hyde, I told you I do whatever you want me to.
Duke, *wondering*. You like me that much?
Kate. More than that. (*They kiss.*)

(*The lights are on them now.*)

Mary. For the ladies in the audience I'd like to introduce a great philosopher, Mr. Duke Hyde.

(*The audience applauds. Duke stands, then sits down.*)

Jean. And now, a medley of our hits.

(*They begin singing.*)

(*Lights fade out.*)

(*Lights are up outside of the hotel. Duke and Kate are waiting for Larry. A bum approaches Duke.*)

Bum. Mr. Hyde—it is you, I know. Please, please help me, Mr. Hyde.
Duke. Who are you? How do you know me?
Bum. I was a friend of your father before he—
Duke, *interrupts him by getting into car which Larry has pulled up in a street walker passes by and sees Kate.*
Street Walker. Kate Goldberg… I see you're doing all right.

(*Larry drives off.*)

(*Lights fade on the Bum and the crowd in front of the hotel.*)

(*Lights are on Larry driving.*)
LARRY. I'm sorry, Mr. Hyde, but that was not your dog.

(*Lights fade out.*)

(*Lights up in Duke's apartment. Duke and Kate are kissing.*)

KATE. Let's go to bed…
DUKE, *roughly*. No… (*He moves away from her.*)
KATE, *gently*. Are you all right? Do you want me?
DUKE, *a pause*. Do I want you? (*He smiles softly.*)
KATE. Then why don't you act like you do.
DUKE, *goes to piano, plays "Satin Doll"—then stops*. Kate, I'm not all human.
KATE. That I know.
DUKE, *jumps from piano seat*. But you couldn't know. (*He goes to bard, pours a drink then lights a stick of pot.*) Kate, my father was a mad man. (*He pauses.*) Both my grandfather and my father experimented with all kinds of drugs. I'm part wolf.
KATE, *laughs hysterically*. Wolf…wolf…
DUKE. Stop it—
KATE, *continues laughing*. Okay.

(*He starts to laugh and can't stop.*)

KATE, *starts to pull her clothes off*. A wolf man. Oh, Duke, I love you. (*Pulling her clothes off.*)
DUKE, *taking another drink*. I know, yes, I know… (*He pulls his clothes off.*)

(*They get in bed.*)

(*Lights fade.*)

Kate, *almost out.* A wolf man…
Duke. Are you asleep already? (*Kate is out.*) She's out…

(*Music comes up. Duke's hand begins to change to a "wolf" hand. Kate turns over and her hands touches the wolf hand, then Duke's face changes to a wolf face.*)

Duke, *getting out of bed.* Ar-ar-ar, ar-ar…
Kate, *awaking.* Turn that stupid music off…
Duke, *continues with "wolf" sounds.* Ar-ar-ar…

(*Kate turns around, sees Duke's face, then tries to get out of the bed, screaming for her life. Duke grabs her, kills her, the blood stemming all over the bed. The doorbell begins to ring. Duke runs into another room, then hides in the bathroom.*)

(*Lights are on Larry, putting key in the door lock.)*

Larry, *entering.* Mr. Hyde, are you here?

(*He goes into the bedroom, see Kate's body and blood all over the bed. As he turns around, Duke has come in and grabs him, throws him to the floor.*)

Larry, *not believing.* No, God, oh no!

(*Duke kills him.*)

(*Lights out.*)
(*The next day. Duke gets morning newspaper from outside his apartment door. Reads headlines: "Two Bodies Found in Trunk at Fifth Avenue and Fifty-Seventh Street."*)

Duke, *takes paper inside.* What—

(*He dashes to the bar, pours a drink then continues reading the paper. He puts paper down, hurries to the telephone to call his mother.*)

(*Lights on Duke's other at her telephone.*)

MOTHER. Hello, son. Did you have a nice night out? (*A pause.*) I'm speaking at the University of Texas, and I want you to come with me as a guest speaker. We leave tomorrow.

(*Lights on Duke at telephone.*)

DUKE. But, Mother, did you see today's paper?

(*Light on Duke and his mother.*)

MOTHER. No, darling. Why?

DUKE, *dully.* Two people were murdered… And I did it. I killed those two people… (*He breaks off.*)

MOTHER, *sorrowfully.* Oh, son, you didn't… You couldn't. Juts forget it—tell no one. Will you come with me to Texas?

DUKE, *shouting.* No, no…no, Mother, I can't.

MOTHER, *gravely.* All right, son. Will you have dinner with me at the house when I return? We must talk about you and your father's ways.

DUKE, *resigned.* Yes, Mother. But don't you think I should see a doctor?

MOTHER, *a sharp cry.* No. Don't do anything until I return from Texas. (*She hangs up.*)

(*Light out.*)

(*Lights up at Tommy Smedley's on East Fiftieth Street. A bar*)

(*Duke parks his car then enters the bar. It is full of girls both white and black. As Duke enters, they turn to look at him. Dan walks up to Duke.*)

DAN. Hi, fellow. What brings you down town?

DUKE, *simply*. I wanted some greens and corn bread.

DAN. Greens…(*smiling*) They are out of sight. Here, come over to my table. That dog bitch, Doris, is with me…

DUKE, *as he and Dan walk to table*. Hello, there. I'm Duke Hyde…

DORIS, *softly*. Oh yes, I heard all about you… You can drink more than me.

DUKE, *quietly*. Dan must have told you about me.

DORIS, *smiling*. Yes, yes, he has.

DAN, *to Duke*. I've got some good H.

DUKE. Forget it. (*Looking at a passing figure.*) Who is that lady that just passed by?

DORIS. Oh, her. That's Sandy… (*She pauses.*) You dig her?

DUKE. Not really. I was just thinking…

DORIS, *a faint smile*. Mr. Hyde, I hear you drink blood.

DAN, *quickly*. You fool—You talk too much.

DUKE, *stands*. Well, I must be going.

(*Sandy walks past the table.*)

SANDY, *to Duke*. Hello there, honey. Would you like some of my blood? (*She laughs and goes to the bar.*)

DAN. But, Duke, what about the Greens and—

DUKE, *interrupting*. See you later, Dan. Stop by and bring the H.

(*He walks out of the restaurant.*)

(*Lights on Sandy looking after Duke.*)

(*Lights on Duke getting into his car and driving off. He stops for a red light—his hands turns into the "wolf" hand. He drives through the red light and stops the car on the other side of the street. His hand has turned back to a human hand. The car's radio is playing some peculiar music Duke drives off as lights fade.*)

(*That same evening about eleven o'clock, Duke is leaving the Paramount Movie Theatre on Broadway at Sixty-First Street. Lights on him as he crosses Central Park West on Sixty-First Street and goes into Central*

Park. An ugly old woman notices him and smiles at him. He smiles back at her. Suddenly he feels something happening to him…)

(*A fire truck passes going up Central Park West. Lights on truck, then lights back on Duke, his face that of a "wolf" man.)*

(*The old woman sees this change and tries to scream, but no sound comes out and she faints, Duke runs to hide, feels his face and finds that the "wolf" face is gone. He goes over to where the old woman is lying, slaps her face until she comes to.*)

OLD WOMAN, *looks at him fearfully*. No… Oh, it's you. But I saw—

DUKE, *interrupts gently*. You fainted… Are you all right now?

OLD WOMAN, *getting up*. I'm all right. I saw a "wolf" man—(*remembering*)—it was you.

Duke, *quietly*. You must be sick. Let me help you.

OLD WOMAN, *confused*. I must be mad. (*She lets Duke help her as she gets up*.)

DUKE. What are you doing here in the park at this hour? Don't you believe what you hear on TV and what you read in the papers?

OLD WOMAN. I never look at TV and I stopped reading the papers when the dodgers moved to Los Angeles.

DUKE. My car is parked across the street. Can I give you a lift home?

OLD WOMAN, *happily*. No, but there's a party up the street (*she points*)—a crazy party. Why don't you come with me? (*She laughs idiotically.*)

DUKE, *as they walk to car*. What types of people will be at the party?

OLD WOMAN, *still laughing, stupidly*. Don't worry, you'll love it. There'll be all kinds of freaks at the mad house—my sister's house.

(*Lights fade slowly as they get in Duke's car and drive off swiftly. The old woman is still laughing.*)

(*Lights up as Duke rings doorbell of house where the party is being held. Very loud music is coming from there. A blind man opens the door and a black cat runs out.*)

Old Woman, *to blind man.* Hello… This is my sister's home.

(*They walk into a mad house: A long haired freak is dancing on the couch, several girls are dancing together, a seven-foot-tall black man is the waiter. The old woman continues to laugh. Then to Duke.*)

Old Woman. Do you take dope?
Duke, *calmly.* Do I take dope? Indeed I do…
Old Woman. Come with me… (*Pulls Duke by the hand into another room where a group of people are smoking pot, shooting up H, and drinking gin.*)
Duke, *happy now.* Gin… That's what I want.
Old Woman, *laughing crazily.* Gin and dope.
Duke, *drinking.* Yes…

(*In the center of the floor is a long-haired freak with a large dog, a man with a long cut on his face, a one-legged man, a heavy fat girl wearing hot pants, and a French lady—her face covered with a veil, and two seven-foot-tall pimps standing over a bed talking to a young girl.*)

Old Woman. We all are beings—like the spirits—and we are spirits just like you, black, yellow, all of us, I get everything I want. See my foot… (*she holds her cut foot up.*) I was on a magic mission—all of us were there—I didn't freak out. I told the doctor at the hospital how to fix it—and he did. (*Sadly.*) Yes, I do feel sad. (*She looks at Duke.*) You look like a Cancernian. My moon is in Cancer (*happily*), Mother Cancer.
Duke. No… I'm a Scorpion.
Sister. And what is your name?
Duke. Duke Hyde.

(*They all break out in laughter.*)

Sister, *continues.* Who did you come with? Was it by magic?
Old Woman. Sister, darling, he came with me—he's a "wolf" man.

SISTER. Yes, I'll bet. And stop calling me your sister, you ugly old bitch.

DUKE, *enjoying this*. This sure is a mad house, (*to sister*) and I think you are very intelligent.

SISTER, *shouting*. I can dance, sing, write—all of those things. (*A pause.*) Give me a drink. (*Continues.)* And my friend here, she got shot the same night I cut my foot, and it was the full moon, I don't work, my rent is paid, people come here and want to give me money and all that nonsense, but I turn them down, I put them out of my home—with all those negative feelings. Some come just to see me. So let it be. (*She laughs.*)

DUKE. Oh, excuse me… (*Goes to the bathroom, finds old woman there.*)

OLD WOMAN. Come on in. You've got nothing I haven't seen.

(*Duke enters, closes the door. Lights on them in bathroom.*)

OLD WOMAN. Let's shoot up.

DUKE, *smiling*. No, let's snuff it.

OLD WOMAN. Good—Anyway is good. (*Duke snuffs, then the old woman snuffs. Then Duke urinates. Old woman laughs crazily again.*)

DUKE, *his mood changing*. Do you live here with your sister?

OLD WOMAN. No, I live in the street.

(*Duke's hand changes to a "wolf" hand—then his head changes to a "wolf" head. The old woman, putting lipstick on sees him in the mirror, drops the lipstick.*)

(*Duke grabs her by the neck and kills her.*)

(*He puts head in the toilet bowl. He opens the bathroom door, looking like a "wolf" man, closes the door again, and looks at himself in the mirror and immediately changes back to a human. He walks out of bathroom and out of house.*)

(*Lights out.*)

(*Lights on.*)

SISTER, *still talking.* I can't believe what is going on! I see my blood in the toilet bowl. (*She gets up, goes in another room where she perches one bird on each hand and goes to the bathroom, opens door, laughing, then calls.*) You crazy sister! Come here, everybody, come to the bathroom and see an old woman with her head in the toilet bowl…

(*They all come to see and they laugh loudly.*)

(*Sister pulls the old woman's hair and sees blood on the old woman's neck and her eyes are wide open. Sister screams. Party members all scream.*)

(*Lights on all.*)

(*Lights fade out.*)

(*The next week. Duke is at a doctor's office.*)

(*Lights on Duke.*)

DUKE, *crying out.* Doctor Smoth, I'm mad. I should be killed. I'm a wolf man. (*He pauses.*) Doctor, I shoot LSD—drink Gin—and shoot H. almost every day. I don't see how I can go on living. (*He pulls doctor to him.*) Help me, help me…

DOCTOR. Please, Mr. Hyde. How did you cone to me?

DUKE, *whispering.* That little old man on Fiftieth Street. The one that talks to everyone who passes on Broadway and Fiftieth Street.

DOCTOR. But my office is closed, and I am leaving for Washington.

DUKE. Doctor, I have money. I have already killed three people. Didn't you read about it in the papers.

DOCTOR, *hesitates.* No… I can't keep up with all this madness in New York. I'm a busy man, and when I have any time I have three children—

DUKE, *interrupts.* My father was a wolf man and it's in my blood. (*He begins to cry.*) I have read that there is help for me and you can help me… You must have heard of my father, Dr. Hyde. There's all kinds of books written about him. (*He is desperate.*) Please help me, doctor!

DOCTOR, *looks at Duke.* This is madness. Your father was the great Dr. Hyde.

DUKE. One of them—there are at least twenty-five Dr. Hydes—(*a pause*)—and all relatives of mine.

DOCTOR, *his face set, shakes his head.* No. If I start treating you there will be more mad dogs coming to my office. (*A pause.*) And I have a family that I want to be safe and happy. (*Quietly.*) No, I can't help you. (*He opens the office door.*) Now, Mr. Hyde, will you please leave—

DUKE. I've got plenty of money to pay you. (*then desperate*) You've got to, or (*wildly, he grabs a sword from the wall and without a word stabs the doctor in the neck, kills him. He types a note which reads: "I can't be the doctor I wanted to be, so, forgive me," and puts it on the desk.*)

(*Lights fade.*)

DUKE, *cries softly*. Mother, mother…

(*Lights out.*)

(*Lights up at May's apartment. May and Sandy are talking about Pimps and the New York Police.*)

SANDY. May, do you know every time you walk outside there's a cop asking some damn question like are you working this block or the other—

MAY. You should be in Hollywood, sweetheart.

SANDY, *interested.* Why California? Is it healthier there than in New York?

MAY. Healthier and the pimps out there are better and look better and take care of themselves much better than these here.

SANDY, *smiles.* Then that's where I'm going.

MAY, *gets up from chair.* You can stay or leave, as you wish, but I'd better get some rest.

SANDY. Rest?

MAY. Yes, rest, I had a heavy night.

SANDY, *eating a candy bar.* About Los Angeles, May. Do you know many people in Hollywood?

MAY. Yes, I do.

SANDY. I'm sick of giving my money to some men.

MAY, *lying down on a couch.* Do you have any grass?

SANDY. No, but what about that Duke Hyde. Maybe—

MAY, *interrupts.* Duke, no. He's been acting like a wild man, lately.

SANDY. Have you ever gone to bed with him? (*May does not answer.*) Do you know that I made $750 last night and that no-good black MF of mine told me that he didn't want it?

MAY, *jumps up.* What? Didn't want it? (*She laughs.*) That sounds like some of that 1950 pimp stuff. Do you have the money?

SANDY. I put it in the bank.

MAY, *surprised.* Bank? You've got a bank account?

SANDY. Hell, yes, (*She hesitates.*) He told me not to come home until I get a grand. I've been thinking, May, and I think I'll leave this city and go to California.

MAY, *somberly.* You mean, get out of New York? But you can't run away from a pimp.

SANDY. Oh, I'm not going to run, I'm going to take my time. (*Coldly.*) Besides, he doesn't do too much for me anymore.

MAY. About the grass—why don't you go over to Duke's apartment and ask him to give me about five quarts.

SANDY. Okay, you know, it's been three weeks since we had an affair and it was like having a trick. (*A pause.*) You know you can buy a dead man for fifty cents.

MAY. For less than that on Forty-Second Street.

SANDY, *laughing.* Forty-Second Street! You're too much. What about you, May? How do you do without a pimp—a man?

MAY. Please… A pimp is a business and I think I can run my business better than any man… Go get the grass.

SANDY. I'm going. (*She leaves.*)

(*Lights on Sandy as she walks to Duke's apartment. She rings bell.*)

DUKE. Who is it?

SANDY. Sandy—from May's apartment.

DUKE, *opens door.* Oh, it's you… Come in.

SANDY. May said she'd like some grass if you have any.

DUKE, *as they walk to the bar.* Yes, are you following me? This is the third time I've seen you in two days.

SANDY. May and I are good friends and I just want to help her, that's all.

DUKE, *reaches behind the bar, gives Sandy the grass.* Here you are. And come and see me sometime.

SANDY, *takes grass.* Thank you, I will, (*she smiles at Duke.*) Do you know how fine a gentleman you are?

DUKE, *grinning.* Thank you, Madame. No—and yes…

(*They walk to door.*)

(*Lights out.*)

(*Lights up at Duke's Mother's house in Westchester, New York. Fran and Mother are having coffee.*)

FRAN. Mrs. Hyde, about last night… I agree with you about Shakespeare and Langston Hughes. Their talents are along the same line.

MOTHER. My dear child, you are just like my son.

FRAN. In what way?

MOTHER. In not thinking as much as you should! Incidentally, why don't you call Duke. He would be surprised to hear your voice.

FRAN, *quietly*. Do you think so?

MOTHER. I know so. Here is his number, 781–6000.

FRAN, *lights on Fran.* (*Goes to phone, dials a number.*) Hello, Duke? Hello, you can't hear me? Hello, I can hear you… I'll call back, hang up. (*She dials again.*)

MOTHER. That New York City telephone company. Something is always wrong with their phones.

FRAN, *lights still on Fran, in phone.* Hello, Duke? It's Fran… Yes, I came back with your mother. Yes, I'm here with her. She's fine. Don't you want to talk to her? (*A pause as Fran listens.*) Okay—Bye, now. (*She hangs up, is ill at ease.*)

MOTHER. I wanted to talk to him, Fran. What's wrong? You look upset. What happened? Was he talking that wolf talk?

FRAN, *hesitantly*. Yes, he said it was too much and nobody would help him, Mrs. Hyde. (*She rises, moves about.*) Is the Hyde family from the old English family of Dr. Hyde?

MOTHER. Yes, darling, didn't you know that?

FRAN. No. I once knew a man by the name of Raphael Hyde…

MOTHER, *smiling*. Oh, poor Raphael. You see, the Hyde family is honeycombed with secret tunnels—(*she stops*)—there's no need to whisper, anymore. This house is very old, the walls are two feet thick on each side, and Duke—(*she stops talking.*)

FRAN, *anxious*. What about Duke? He asked me to marry him and I turned him down. If there is anything I can do to make him happy, I'll do my best.

MOTHER. You had better not see Duke (*with alarm.*)

(*Fran looks at mother.*)

(*Lights slowly fade out.*)

(*Lights on Duke walking out of church and on Fran walking on the other side of the street, Fran sees Duke and calls out:*)

FRAN, *calling.* Duke, oh Duke... (*He stops and looks over.*) It's Fran, Duke... (*She crosses over to where Duke has stopped on the church steps.*)

(*Lights on both of them.*)

DUKE, *surprised.* Fran! I didn't mean to (*he stops then.*)—How did you know I was here?

FRAN, *smiling.* It must be my third eye...

DUKE. Must be. (*He kisses her.*)

FRAN. How are you?

DUKE. Not too cool...

FRAN. What do you mean?... That you're not working? (*A pause.*) Duke, you know that's not good for a man like you. (*They walk to Duke's car.*)

DUKE, *as they get in car.* Have you heard about Larry's getting killed?

(*Lights on them as they drive off Fran lights up a stick of pot.*)

FRAN, *distressed.* No, I didn't know. When did this happen? Your mother told me you no longer had a driver, but (*sadly*)—I'm so sorry, Duke.

DUKE, *quietly.* Forget it... But you know how close Larry and I were. (*He changes the subject.*) How about having some lunch?

FRAN. I didn't come here to have lunch...

DUKE. What did you mean by that?

FRAN, *passing him the pot.* How's your sex life? (*Can't you talk about it anymore?*)

(*Duke stops the car for a red light on Forty-Second Street at Broadway.*)

(*A bum approaches car, asks Duke for a quarter. Duke gives him a quarter. The light changes and they drive off packing across the street.*) (*They get out of car.*)

DUKE. You get what you ask for, honey. (*Fran laughs.*) (*They proceed down Forty-Second Street toward Eight Avenue.*)

FRAN. Duke, I didn't come three thousand miles just to walk on Forty-Second Street. What is wrong?

DUKE. My mind is slowing up.

FRAN. Slowing up? How can you say that? (*They stop to watch a fight between two men—one, a Fag. Police come quickly and stop the fight.*)

DUKE. The dirty bitch! (*Angrily.*)

FRAN. Why are you so angry, Duke?

DUKE, *furious now.* Will you get your white ass away from me and stop asking so many damned questions? (*Loudly.*) Go on, get going…

(*The policemen are looking at Duke.*)

(*Lights fade on cops.*)

(*Then lights fade out on Fran, who is standing, like a lost child on Forty-Second Street. Duke walks away from her.*)

(*Twelve midnight.*)

(*Lights up at Small's, in Harlem. They pan to Duke seated alone at the bar. Soon, May and Sandy enter. Duke's head is down.*)

MAX, *seeing Duke at the bar.* There's your lover boy, Sandy… Duke Hyde. (*She points to him.*)

SANDY, *happily.* Oh, it is Duke. (*They walk to the bar.*)

MAY. Hi, Duke…

SANDY. Hello, Mr. Hyde. (*Duke rises, turns to them.*)

DUKE. Well, well, this is a surprise. (*The bartender brings glasses and a bottle of gin as they all sit. Lights go to the band stan and to a singer with a small band. Lights back on Duke and the two girls.*)

SANDY. Do you come here very Saturday night?

MAY. Don't be silly, Sand, this man is part of Harlem's new rock center—he goes everywhere.

(*Lights on band, then on Duke.*)

DUKE. May, you look out of this world. (*He looks at Sandy.*) And as for you, Sandy—what is it—beauty night? (*They all laugh.*)

SANDY, *still laughing*. What you see is what you're gonna get. (*They all laugh again.*)

(*Lights on band and singer as song ends. Then, lights on Duke and the two girls, as Dan walks into the bar.*)

DAN. Say, Duke, I've got what you want. But I see you're doing okay. (*Continues.*) Hi, May… Hi, Sandy. See you cat's later… There's a party going at 1415 Central Park West, Apartment 11A.

DUKE, *he and girls get up to leave*. No, thanks. We've got our own party going.

DUKE, *laughing*. With your own bad, black asses. (*They all laugh. Duke and girls exit. They go to Duke's car.*)

(*Lights are on Dan at bar.*)

DAN, *to bartender*. Hi, Mack…

(*Music plays as lights slowly fade out.*)

(*Lights up on Duke, May, and Sandy entering Duke's apartment building. They are all quite high on pot. They enter elevator, leave on May's floor, enter May's apartment as lights black out.*)

(*Lights up in May's apartment. They are all seated on a king-size bed.*)

MAY, *coy*. Make yourselves at home.

SANDY, *looks at Duke*. Now, May, don't you worry about this good-looking man. (*She leaves room.*) This is home…

(*They all laugh.*)

(*The television set is on.*)

DUKE, *to May*. Turn that off, please. (*May does so.*) Thanks, honey…

SANDY, *re-enters room with nothing but her panties on*. Hey, Duke, let's shoot some stuff.

MAY. Yeah, that's talking.

DUKE, *rises from bed, pulls of his clothes*. Sandy, what made you get in street life.

SANDY, *going to Duke*. Why am I in this business—street life? (*She laughs.*) Say, what is this going to be? A Mamma and Daddy talk?

DUKE, *his clothes off now*. Something like that.

MAY. Like group therapy… (*She gets into bed with all her clothes on.*)

DUKE. You're first, May. Tell us about yourself.

MAY. Me?

DUKE. Yes, you're first, then Sandy.

SANDY. Come on, bitch, talk.

MAY, *calmly*. Why am I a bitch?

DUKE. Because that's a good starter.

MAY. Let's shoot up, first.

DUKE. Okay with me. (*They proceed with the stuff. Rock music is heard. Duke continues*:) I need a drink.

MAY. Help yourself, Duke, you know where it is.

SANDY, *feeling high*. Come on, May. Tell us about your sex life.

MAY. Okay. First, I'm my own boss. What the hell do I need a man to tell me how to make love? (*She pauses.*) And when?

MAY, *continues*. My mother was a junkie and my old man was a male whore. I've got no brothers or sisters. (*Coldly.*) Why do we all have it so hard?

(*Lights pan to Sandy and Duke. Sandy is embracing Duke.*)

DUKE, *interested*. Come on, May, keep talking. Tell us more about your life, your past. It's something like mine.

MAY. Oh yeah?

DUKE. Well, I have no brothers or sisters, either.

SANDY. My old lady made love like crazy—I've got five sisters and five half-brothers.

MAY, *looks at Duke*. Duke, if you were a pimp, Maybe I would let you pimp for me.

DUKE. That's enough, May.

MAY. I don't know why I said that—guess the Devil made me say it. (*A pause.*) Say, that's some good stuff. (*She points at the gin bottle and the spoon, used for the dope.*) We must be nuts, to do this to ourselves…

SANDY, *kisses Duke*. Now can I tell more about my life?

MAY. All right, honey—this is your life. (*They all smile.*)

SANDY, *continues*. I sold my body when I was—ten. That's right, I was ten. I went with Billy Beergold to a movie, to see Lena Horne in "Stormy Weather." Billy wanted to kiss me. I told him I would do more than kiss if he would give me five dollars. And I did!… I started selling myself then and I haven't stopped yet.

(*Lights begin to fade.*)

(*May has passed out.*)

SANDY. Duke, she's out. Tell me about yourself.

MAY, *coming to*. I'm not out yet.

SANDY, *embracing Duke*. Come on, Duke, tell us.

DUKE. Cool it.

SANDY. Duke, don't you want me?

MAY. He said to cool it, you bitch.

SANDY, *flairs up*. How can you be so cool when this man is the same room with us?

MAY. You heard him, Sandy.

DUKE. Okay, girls, that's enough. (*They are all in bed, now.*) (*Continues.*) My father died before I was born. But I had a good life, as a child. (*A pause.*) I wonder if he knew that I would be what I am—a "wolf."

MAY, *almost asleep*. Okay, wolf man… Keep talking…

DUKE. When I think about it, it seems fantastic. (*A pause.*) I better go. (*He sees that both girls have passed out.*) (*To himself.*) It can't be—(*He looks at his hand which is turning into a "wolf" hand and then feels his face, which is turning into a "wolf" face.*)

(*Lights pan to May, as she turns over and sees Duke as the wolf man, she jumps up from bed. Duke jumps up after her as she tries to get out of the room. May runs around the room, jumps across the bed and wakes Sandy.*)

(*Lights are on Sandy, as she awakens and sees Duke holding May by the neck, killing her. Sandy faints. Duke lifts her from the bed and shoots some dope into her arm, killing Sandy also, from an OD.*)

(*Duke has now returned to a human, he goes to apartment door and looks in the hall. There is no one there.*)

(*Lights are on Duke going into his apartment, music is up.*)

(*Lights begin to fade, flash to the dead girls, then lights out.*)

(*The next day.*)

(*Duke, his mother and Fran are having soul food lunch at Miss Lacey's on Fifty-Seventh Street.*

MOTHER, *rather faintly.* Duke, you've got to go to Los Angeles for me. I won't be able to make it.

DUKE, *concerned.* But Mother,—

MOTHER, *interrupts.* Don't "but Mother" me, son. I'm just not up to going.

DUKE, *anxious.* Are you feeling all right?

MOTHER. Well—(*she pauses*)—you need to get out of New York City.

FRAN. Your mother told me you haven't given a talk in six months, Duke.

DUKE. That's right.

FRAN. But why not, Duke?

DUKE. I told you I—(*he stops.*)

MOTHER. This will be for the Board of Health at UCLA and you'll be able to see some of your old friends.

DUKE, *coldly*. What friends?

FRAN, *rises*. I'd better call to see if I can get reservations to leave here. (*She leaves room.*)

DUKE. When is she leaving, Mother?

MOTHER. Some time tonight. (*Changing subject.*) Duke, you killed two girls last night.

DUKE, *evading*. Please, Mother, why don't you call the police if you know all this.

MOTHER, *hurt*. Your father would be so heartbroken.

DUKE, *tearfully*. Oh, Mother, I'm so unhappy.

MOTHER, *crying softly*. I know, Son...(*firmly.*) That's why you must go to Los Angeles. I've already called the dean and said that you would come in my place.

DUKE, *almost screaming*. You didn't... You didn't... (*Fran enters room.*) Fran, when are you leaving?

FRAN. I've got one hour to make it. Will you take me to the airport, Duke?

DUKE, *resigned*. Yes, and I'm going to Los Angeles as mother asked me to.

MOTHER, *happy*. That's what I like about the Hyde men—they all obey...

(*Fran and Duke kiss mother and leave Miss Lacey's. Mother looks after them.*)

(*Lights fade as waiter comes over to mother's table.*)

WAITER. Is there anything else? (*Mother slumps over in chair—dead of a heart attack.*) Mrs. Hyde... (*He touches her arm.*)... Are you all right? (He sees she is dead.) Oh, no, she is dead… *(Shouts.)* Miss Lacey, Miss Lacey. (*He runs to phone to call for an ambulance. Miss Lacey goes to mother's table, takes mother's purse.*)

MISS LACEY, *aloud.* Isn't this something! She had to die here.

(*Lights fade at the sound of ambulance, then12lights out.*)

(*Lights up on airplane. Fran and Duke are in the lounge, having a drink.*)

FRAN. Your mother is a wonderful lady, Duke. (*She is interrupted by a voice from the intercom.*)

(*Voice.*)

(*Mr. Duke Hyde, Mr. Duke Hyde… Please return to your seat. Do you hear me? Please return to your seat… There is an air cable for Mr. Duke Hyde…*)

DUKE, *as he and Fran go back to their seats.* What is this seat bit?
(*A Stewart is standing at his seat.*)

STEWART. Mr. Hyde? (*He hands Duke the air cable—waits for him to read it.*)

DUKE, *reading cable.* But how—when—we just left her…(*he sits, sobs.*)

FRAN, *taking cable.* (*She reads.*) But it can't be. We—(*she sits and takes Duke's arm.*)

STEWART. I'm very sorry, Mr. Hyde. Can I get you something?

DUKE, *still crying.* Oh, Fran, you are all I have. Fran—(*to Stewart.*) No, thanks. (*Stewart leaves.*)

FRAN. Don't you want a drink? Some gin?

DUKE. I can't (*a slight pause.*) If I drink gin, something terrible will happen.

FRAN. Duke, I'm going back to New York. She was so sweet, so good.

DUKE, *his eyes getting red from crying.* Fran, my father was a—(*he stops.*)

FRAN. What, Duke?
DUKE. Fran, oh, Fran, what will I do now? (*He cries out.*)

(*The other passengers are staring at them as lights begin to fade.*)

DUKE. Oh, God… Help me…

(*Lights are out.*)

(*Three weeks later: Duke's apartment in New York City.*)

(*Lights up on Fran and Duke in bed.*)

DUKE. I feel like a new man. (*He pauses, looks at Fran.*) You know something? I think mother was sticking pins in a voodoo doll—making me kill!
FRAN. Why, Duke Hyde?
DUKE, *feeling his head.* My head is like new. I don't have any more pains and no more bad dreams.
FRAN. You talk like a child.
DUKE. Fran, I'm a murderer—I killed.
FRAN, *smiles.* You're crazy, Duke.
DUKE, *shakes his head assenting.* That I am—that I am. (*The doorbell rings. Fran puts on housecoat, goes to answer. Sees John.*)
FRAN. Oh, come in, John.
DUKE, *calls.* Who is it?
FRAN. It's John. (*To John.*) He's in bed, but come in.
JOHN. I'm sorry to disturb you but I had to see him. (*Duke enters room. Fran leaves them together.*)
JOHN. Duke, I'm sorry about your mother—
DUKE, *interrupting.* Okay, forget it. What do you want?
JOHN. I've got some good H and LSD.
DUKE, *distressed.* You know damn well you should have called me.
JOHN. But, Duke—
DUKE, *interrupting.* I told you never to drop by without calling me… Now, get out of here, you white bastard. (*He holds door open.*)

JOHN. All right, man. But did you hear that they found May and Sandy—

DUKE, *holding his head.* What do you mean?

JOHN. They were found dead. They had been dead for a week.

DUKE, *quietly.* Oh, no. That's too bad. Will you leave, now. I smoke only pot, now.

JOHN, *laughing.* I can't believe that you—

DUKE, *interrupts, almost screaming.* Will you go now?

JOHN, *at open door.* Take it easy, man.

DUKE, *pushes John out door.* You white fag… Get out.

(*Lights out.*)

(*Lights on Duke driving down Seventh Avenue in his Rolls Royce. He passes a large number, in a group of prostitutes, most of them black. Lights pan to girls. Then lights go to Duke. Duke gets out of car, goes to a hotdog stand where he purchases some food. A girl walks up to him.*)

GIRL. Hi, honey, how about some fun?

DUKE. No, thanks, baby… I like boys.

GIRL. My name is Ruth. What's yours? I can call my pimp for you.

DUKE. My name's Duke—Duke Hyde.

RUTH. I say, Duke—that's a good name. Are you a pimp?

DUKE. Yes…(*he smiles.*) No, I'm not.

RUTH. You better dig me, honey, because I don't date black men, as a rule.

DUKE. Why is it that you girls don't like to date black men?

RUTH. The only black man I date is my man.

DUKE. Then why ask me?

RUTH. Because you look like a good John.

DUKE. Some other time. (*He starts for his car.*)

(*Voice of girl.*)

(*Here comes the cops… You'd better run.*)

(*The prostitutes start running down the avenue—one loses a shoe, one loses her wig—screaming as they run from the police. Ruth follows Duke into car.*)

DUKE, *laughing*. That's funny.
RUTH. I don't think so. What's so funny about it.
DUKE. What's your old man gonna say when he finds out you got in a car with a black man?
RUTH, *moves close to Duke*. Forget about him, honey.
DUKE. Okay. (*They drive off.*)

(*From Duke and fade to the cops and the girls. The cops grab two of the girls, pull them to police car. Girls call the cops all kinds of dirty words and names.*)

(*Lights go to Duke's car parking at his apartment. John passes by in his cab, sees Duke with Ruth, he calls from his cab.*)

JOHN, *stops cab, calls to Duke*. Hey, man… I see you know how to pick then.
DUKE. Get moving, John.
JOHN. Can't I come up?
DUKE. No. (*He and Ruth get out of car as John pulls off.*)
RUTH. He must be some kind of a nut.
DUKE. You're telling me. I know that guy.
RUTH. You're funny. (*They walk toward Duke's building.*)
DUKE. Don't tell me that.
RUTH. But you are…(*they reach the front of Duke's building.*) Oh, you live in the same building that my sister lives in—(*she catches herself*)—I mean that my sister used to live in. They found her dead—she and May.
DUKE. *stops, looks at her*. Oh… You knew May?
RUTH. Sure. She was a good kid. But that Sand, I wanted to kill her. She was a no-good bitch. But that's life—some people are good and some are bad.

DUKE. Let's not go up. Let's go in the park.

RUTH, *shocked.* The park?

DUKE. Or, let's go to Tommy Smalls. I'd like some soul food.

RUTH. No, I'm sorry, but my old man hangs out there. (*They are standing on Central Park West.*)

DUKE. Who is your pimp?

RUTH. You wouldn't know him.

DUKE. What's his name?

RUTH. Dan Dean… (*Duke bursts out laughing.*) What's so goddam funny? (*Duke is still laughing as…*)

(*Lights out.*)

(*Lights up inside Duke's apartment. Ruth is in bed, nude.*)

RUTH. I'd better be going.

DUKE. Why the rush?

RUTH. I've got to make some "bread" money.

DUKE. Stay here. I'll give you a yard.

RUTH. A yard?

DUKE. That's right. How about some gin? (*They get out of bed, go to bar. Some idiotic music is playing.*)

RUTH. What do you have—H or Snow?

DUKE. I've got H. No Snow. (*They both are having a gin drink.*) Do you shoot up?

RUTH. Yes, but—(*she pauses.*) Okay, you go first. (*Duke shoots himself, then he shoots Ruth.*)

RUTH. Hey, baby… I feel like getting back in bed. (*She goes to Duke, kisses him.*)

DUKE. That's fine with me. (*They go to the bed and when they reach it, Ruth passes out of an overdose.*)

DUKE. Ruth, Ruth. Goddam it… This bitch is dead. (*He looks at his hand and sees it turning into a "wolf" hand. He feels his face and it has changed into a "wolf" face. He goes to mirror, tries to get his reflection in the mirror then smashes it. Duke begins to change back to a human as a knock is heard on the apartment door.*)

(*Lights fade to outside of door. The cops are there with Duke's lost dog, who is barking incessantly. This time there is more knocking. But Duke does not answer.*)

(*Lights on Duke sitting on a bar stool.*)

(*Lights out.*)

(*Next afternoon.*)

(*Lights up at Duke's apartment. Doorbell rings. It is Doris and Dan. Lights pan to them. Doris knocks on door, thinking doorbell is not working.*)

DORIS. He's gotta be home.
DAN. Oh, Duke could be any place.

(*Lights up on Duke as he goes to door, calling:*)

DUKE, *calling*. Hello... Who in hell is it?
DAN, *outside*. It's Dan.
DUKE, *alarmed*. I told you not to—(*He opens the door. Sees Doris with Dan.*)—Oh, come in.
DAN. I thought you'd like to see Doris.
DORIS, *happily*. Hello, Duke. (*They walk into apartment toward the bar. The bedroom door is closed. Ruth's body is still there.*)

(*Lights go to body—then back to Duke who offers them a seat.*)

DUKE, *sits*. Doris Dee, it's great to see you again. Where have you been?
DORIS, *smiles*. Oh, Los Angeles and—Hong Kong.
DAN. Tell us about Hong Kong...
DORIS. Out of this world... You'd both love it. Dope—Dope—
DUKE, *interrupts*. Doris hasn't changed! You're looking great, baby.
DORIS. But Duke, what is this I hear about you and his wolf stuff?

DUKE. Oh, come on—Dan's nuts... Don't pay any attention to him.

DORIS. But there is something to this werewolf belief. (*Points to Dan.*) Dan himself, he's a wolf. (*They all laugh.*)

DUKE, *gets up*. I'll get some pot. (*He returns, and they light up.*)

DORIS. Good grass.

DAN. That's right. Duke keeps gold.

DUKE, *modestly*. Come on, Dan.

DAN. But it's true, you do.

DORIS. Not only grass but do you still have good coke?

DUKE, *feeling sick*. You know, I haven't been feeling too well, I'm going to start getting more rest.

DORIS, *dreamily*. Good grass...

DAN. You know Ruth—that whore from Seventh Avenue—well, her old man's mad as hell with you, Duke.

DORIS, *getting up*. I have to leave. Dan and I ran into each other at Seventy-Second Street and I wanted to see you, Duke. Be seeing you...(*she leaves apartment.*)

DAN. No, not me... It's white Dan. (*A pause.*) Man, you know, there's a full moon tonight.

(*Lights go to moon.*)

(*An ambulance siren is heard. Duke turns on the television set, and a News Bulletin is just coming on. Lights on TV.*)

TV BROADCASTER. I'm sorry to interrupt this program... The drug addict who killed two people in Times Square has been apprehended... The man, whose name is James Clarke, has admitted he was once a Black Panther. He has been taken to Bellevue Hospital.

DUKE, *turning TV set off.* That makes me mad. Every time there's a murder, it's a Black Panther that does it—

DAN, *interrupts*. It's the full moon, man. (*Changing subject.*) But about Ruth, what time did she leave, Duke? (*Duke does not answer. Dan goes to him.*) Hey, man, hey, about Ruth—when did she leave? Her pimp is burning because she went with you.

DUKE, *his hand to his head.* My heads killing me… Oh, Ruth? She said she was going to see—(*he hesitates*)—Bea Gibson. You know Bea, that big, black bitch who tells your fortune?

DAN. Oh sure… Bea Gibson—she's good.

DUKE. Do you know her address?

DAN. She's on Fiftieth Street. (*He writes the address down on a pad.*)

Oh, man, I can see you've had it. I'll see you later. (*He is ready to go.*)

DUKE. I think I'll go to see Miss Gibson. (*He shakes hands with Dan, who leaves apartment.*)

(Duke *goes to bedroom, puts Ruth's body in a white plastic bag, then puts this bag in a large trunk. He calls for the houseman to put the trunk in his car.*)

(*Lights go to houseman on the telephone.*)

HOUSEMAN. Yes, Mr. Hyde. I'll be right up.

(*Lights out.*)

(*Lights up on Duke. He is driving West on Fifty-Seventh Street toward the Hudson River. It is now about twelve o'clock midnight… Duke reaches river and backs his car up to river. He gets out of car, puts trunk with body in it, on the ground, then pushes trunk into the river. He acts unconcerned, walks back to car and speaks to himself, "Thank you, Jesus"… He drives off quickly.*)

(*Lights fade to Miss Bea Gibson's apartment on Fiftieth Street. Lights are up on Duke and Miss Bea…*)

BEA GIBSON, *reading him.* Sir, you are troubled—very much troubled. There is something in your life that need not be. You have everything one could ever want.

DUKE. Miss Bea, tell me—

BEA GIBSON, *interrupts him.* You have no mother or father. You have no one, only a girlfriend… Her name is Fran. Son, she knows everything about you but don't worry, she loves you and will never let the cat out of the bag. But I see a man in your life—doing you some wrong. You will (*she stops*)—

DUKE, *anxiously.* Will what?

BEA GIBSON, *firmly.* Nothing. That will be twenty-five dollars.

(*Duke pays her, leaves her apartment.*)

(*Lights on Bea Gibson as Duke leaves and she closes the door.*)

(*Lights out.*)

(*Lights up on Duke's apartment as Duke gets out of elevator. He sees Dan in front of the door.*)

DUKE, *upset.* What are you doing here? (*He opens the apartment door.*)

DAN. I want to know about Ruth. (*They both go into Duke's bedroom.*)

DUKE. Will you get out of my life?

DAN, *looks at him, sadly.* Tell me, Duke, what was in that trunk that the houseman put in your car? He told me you drove away with a trunk.

DUKE. A trunk?

DAN. Yes, a trunk… An MD trunk…

DUKE, *goes to bar, pours himself a drink of gin.* Like to have a drink?

DAN, *not answering.* You know, Duke, now I believe you—about all that "wolf" shit you spoke about.

(*He goes into bathroom, leaving the door open. As he turns around to return to room, Duke appears as a "wolf" man. Dan tries to reach the door, fighting furiously toward Duke off. Dan grabs a clock from bedroom wall and hits the "wolf" man a hard blow, then races to get out of the room. Dan is followed by the "wolf" man. He grabs an ice pick that is on a table and as the "wolf" man reaches for his neck, Dan plunges it into the "wolf" man before he is strangled. They both fall on the bed—*

dead! Fran and the police get no response to their continued ringing of the doorbell at Duke's apartment.)

(*The police break the door and they enter. They go to bedroom, see the two men on bed, Duke as the "wolf" man, holding the ice pick and Dan—both dead.*)

ACKNOWLEDGMENT

I WOULD LIKE TO thank Rev, Billy Graman for coming into my life at the age of twelve years old. Teaching me to be with the love of God the rest of my life. So many great people I would like to acknowledge, like Sharman Mark, the producer/director, a great friend of mine who told me my talents compared to Brando, James Earl Jones, Ruby Dee, Richard Burton, MM and Morgan Freeman. When he said that to me, I ran outside of the theater and cried. I have to acknowledge Will Greer and the Walton Family. Will liked my talents so much, when I did Of Mice and Men, I played Crooks. Will played in Of Mice and Men on Broadway with Lee Wolooper, who played Crooks. The day I played Crooks at his theater. Lee Wolooper died, Will said, I was so good I killed Lee. We worked together like Salt and Pepper. I have to acknowledge Mr. Dick Van Dyke for being a fan, working with him on the People's Choice Awards, I was the first black man to sing and act on the People's Choice, the first year of Star Wars and John Wayne. Working with Dick was a joy, we all sang, Put on a happy face, the cast of Singing Impressions. The after was at Chesen, Hollywood's best movie star restaurant. Before the cast was told they were invited, Dick made it known, "If the cast cannot go, I won't go, are you crazy?" I went to the cast party, talking and taking pictures. Thank you Mr. Dick for what you did for my life. Los Angeles Sentinel's, Gertrude Gipson, was the first to call me multi-talented, keeping me in the news. Cindy and Joey Adams, you played a big part in my life in New York. Debbie Verrett, you and Furn Jennings get a Thank you. Betty, Parlene, Phyllis, Sha Jones, Dottie May, Queene, Linda and Lena Horne for being there when I needed family talk.

Jesse Bolero

The Shadow of His Soul

Sit front row center or the balcony rail
On the catwalk or the stage door chair
Out in the lobby or off in the wings
You'll know the moment he's there

Listen from inside the box office cage
Or at the orchestra leader's stand
That unmistakable voice fills the air
It's none other than the Man

When Jesse performs, *you* share the stage,
Sing the lyric, and play out the role
His powerful passion puts you in the cast
In the shadow of his soul

Those of us who have been entertained
By the talent, the charm and quick droll
Of Jesse Bolero, will always applaud
From the shadow of his soul

...Pete Moss 2010

" THE BEGINING "

age 20 walking the Street in Bev. Hills.
when a MGM photograph took
these photo in 1966 and the
Rest is History of me.

AP PHOTO

SHAKING THROUGH: Sen. Joseph Lieberman, above, greets supporters at the Democratic party headquarters in Washington yesterday. Below, Dick Cheney greets Cab Calloway impersonator Jesse Bolero in Las Vegas

BOSTON HERALD TUESDAY, NOVEMBER 7, 2000

DUKE HYDE

Jess Bolero as Cab Calloway

Love you

"UNJUST DO NOT PROSPER"
Jess Bolero --- Baby Lords 1973

James
Jesse

Impressionist – Actor

DUKE HYDE

CAB
Jesse

Roger
Miss World
Jesse

JESSE W. BOLERO

JESSE BOLER

DUKE HYDE

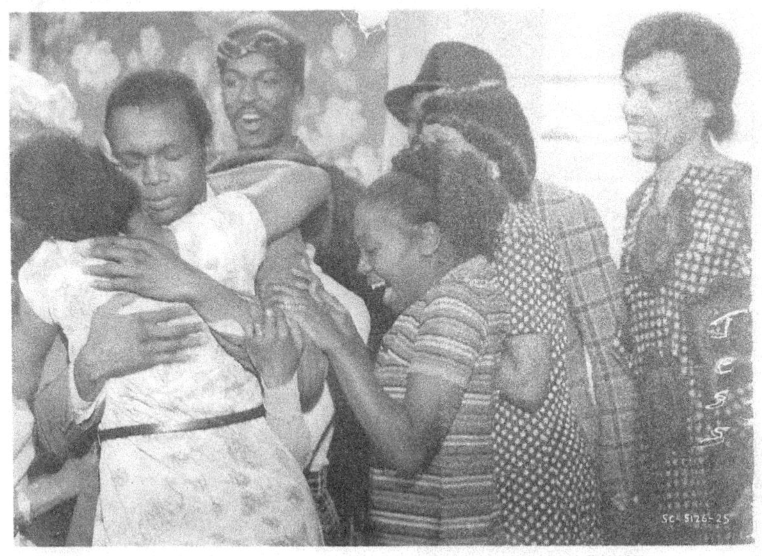

"THE EDUCATION OF SONNY CARSON"

In Color

A Paramount Picture 

JESSE W. BOLERO

1976
Hollywood.
7510 Hwd. Bl.

Jesse Bolero and the Duke

my FATHER AND His Family

Dorthy Boler
DORA
FAYE
JESSE BOLER
Wilmon Boler and Emma Family
and
grandchildren

Jess
POOR JOHN'S BILLIE HOILDAY
CLUB 1958 - NYC
N.Y.C.

People Are Talking About

New York's Jess Bolero and his determination to land the major role in the touring company of Broadway's smash hit, *Hello, Dolly!* Less than 24 hours after undergoing surgery, the comedian slipped out of Roosevelt Hospital, swooped 15 blocks to the St. James Theatre where auditions were in progress, went through the role and cracked up everybody, even the stage hands, leaving them laughing as he returned to his hospital bed. During his entire AWOL stint, Bolero's only clothes were a robe, house slippers and a hospital gown.

Jese Bolero is simply magnificent in an old-time gospel number. As he lectures his flock on the virtues of liberation, he executes minstrel struts of wild invention. He is an inspired comic and a candidate for stardom.

Lena Meets Sir Lady Java At Festive L. A. Birthday Bash

"Unbelievable!" That was Lena Horne's reaction when she first met Sir Lady Java. "He's so feminine, I can't believe he's a man.'

Among the celebrities present were actors Raymond St. Jacques, Stack Pierce, D'Urville Martin, Paul Harris, comedienne, Brenda Verrett, comedian Jess Bolero and singer Ron Townsend.

But the highlight of the evening came when the world's most beautiful woman came face to face with a man who is almost as beautiful—female impersonator Sir Lady Java, who is famous in the L... ...eles area for "her" unique ...ich includes singing, exotic

Theme Of Warm Tribute To Composer

The show was beautifully coordinated by producer Peter Long and co-producer Ed Eckstine, with yeoman service by the production staff, including Jess Bolero, Felicia Jeter, Sid McCoy, Sandy Lovelace, Joe Phillips and Hal DeWindt.

Naturally, the great themes composed by Quincy Jones for outstanding motion pictures were played in tribute to the music

Overcome by emotion, Jones is embraced by veteran screen star Sidney Poitier, one of the many celebrities who appeared in the terrific show that drew 6,500 persons to fill the Shrine Auditorium for moving tribute to composer.

for her book *Zealy* . . . Multi-talented showman Jess Bolero, who sings, dances, mimics and tells funny stories, is doing his things at Johnny Desmond's Wine Cellar . . . is singing praises to TV star

New York BEAT

THE SAN JUAN STAR

The King of the Chinese Slop loosened the cork on the bottle of champagne: Jesse Bolero, actor (he's going to appear in the 'Dutchman' by Leroi Jones), singer (he's a mixture of Billy Eckstine and Arthur Prysock), dancer (he was unchallenged in a Chinese slop contest) impersonator (he makes Louis Armstrong sound like Louie Armstrong...

and especially since Clarence Williams III pulled his coat on how to put on a crazy act with the executives. . . . Paramount biggies are so delighted by Jess Bolero's "happy ... in the current film, *Education Of Sonny Carson*, that they'll build up his role of Sonny's Uncle Red in the already planned sequel. The filming itself has seen greater community ...

ON B'WAY
SHORAN
Jess

Billy Eckstein

BOLERO

To Jesse,
it's been
a long time!
BRENDA RUSSELL

KENN DUNCAN
Miss Alaina Reed

BOLERO'S
STARRING
NICK LA'TOUR
CAFE SOCIETY
MUSICAL
REVUE
STARRING:
Sarah Baldwin
Tawnjai
Lanny Mitchell
Stave Hicks
Tresa Anderson
STARRING:
Jess Bolero
Dennis Rogers
Dian Marshall
Chauncey Roberts
Don Blackwell
A NIGHT OF NOSTALGIA
JESS BOLERO — Producer/Director
Mary Ann Dolcemascolo — Production Chief

JESSE W. BOLERO

Jesse Boler
[illegible] Boler
Willie Jenkins
1959 Don Boler
in Chicago Ill

The Boler
Boys
1960

DR ANDRE V. PRICE
Jess

Best Friend
George T.

DR. GEORGE MINOR
NEPHEW

BEST FRIEND
BRENDA VERRETT

LeNDA
Jess

BEST FRIEND
FERN
JENNINGS

DIBBie MoRgiN
- Jess

Jess
1946
S.M. Beach
Calif

LADIES
Jess
Mr. magic

DEBBIE
REYNOLDS
TEEN AGE IDOL

LANGSTON Hughes WORK
LINCOINCENTER
Jess

JESS AND BAND

Lena and Duke Ellington

Lena and Laurence Olivier

USS MORRIS
HAPPY H FFERS AND Jess

URDAY, OCTOBER 11, 1969

Dream Street

By ROBERT SYLVESTER

The Added Lines ....

A new company of "Hello, Dolly" is being cast to tour this season, and the producer advertised for singers and dancers. A couple of days ago the hopefuls all appeared for the first audition, including one singer and dancer in bathrobe, pajamas and slippers. His name was Jeff Bolero. He explained that he had just sneaked out of Roosevelt Hospital, where he was due for minor surgery. Yes, he got the part . . . Ad in an underground gazette: "Dear Herbert W.: Mother and I forgive you. Please don't come home. Dad." . . . Autumn is definitely here. The boys along Third Ave. have switched to their winter Pucci pants. . . . They sent me tickets to that wife-swapping movie and I'm willing to trade them in. . . . They raffled off 78 buffaloes for $28,640, but, unfortunately, I just herd of it. Ugh! . . . Covered wagons are having a cross-country race. In New York, they'll have to make a circle. . . . A pub for nudists opened in England. Hope they have heated bar stools.

Judy Carne

Petula Clark

* * *

Jesse Ride
Classic
Rolls Royce
Rental
554 CTB

Jesse Ride

Jess
IN
PARIS

DUKE HYDE

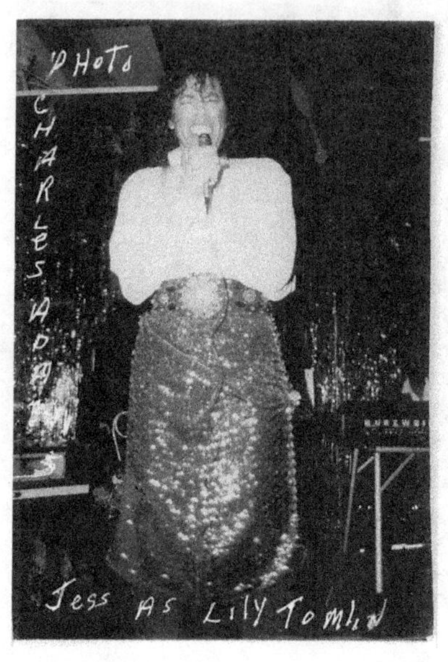
PHOTO
CHARLES
Jess As Lily Tomlin

Jess AT CAESARS PALACE

R.
CHARLES
TINA T.
GEORGE B.
Jess
Hollie
DON

SENATORIAL RECOGNITION

AWARDED TO

Jesse Bolero

WITH APPRECIATION FOR YOUR COMMITMENT AND SERVICE
TO THE CATHOLIC CHARITIES SENIOR COMPANION PROGRAM
AND FOR THE DIFFERENCE YOU MAKE IN OUR COMMUNITY

DECEMBER 9, 2009
DATE

John Ensign
JOHN ENSIGN
UNITED STATES SENATOR

Presented To

JESSE BOLERO

FUNDRAISING FOR THE VETERANS DAY PARADE

For Meritorious and Distinguished Service in Furthering the Aims and Ideals of the Veterans of Foreign Wars of the United States.

Given this 11th day of November, 2007

Commander

Adjutant

Marine Corps League

MARINE CORPS LEAGUE
SEMPER FIDELIS

Certificate of Appreciation

to

Jesse Bolero

The Greater Nevada Detachment of the Marine Corps League extends its deep appreciation for your invaluable and highly-entertaining support of our fund-raising event which was held on April 25, 2010. We salute your patriotic spirit!

Awarded this **21st** *day of* **July, 2010**

Sr. Vice Commandant

Adjutant-Paymaster

FIRST
MODELING
JOB
JESS BoLERO
PHOTO by
John
PATRICK
HART

JESS
BoLERO
Photo by
John P. HART

FIST MODELING
JOB
Photo by
John P. HART

Photo by John P. HART

SOMEONE'S KILLING THE LEGENDS OF JAZZ!!!

WHODUNIT?

...a moving tribute to a bygone era that mesmerizes audiences from beginning to end"

WAS IT BILLIE HOLIDAY? LOUIS JORDAN? LENA HORNE? ETTA JAMES? CAB CALLOWAY? OR THE SUAVE M.C., BILLY GAMBLE?

Perhaps it was the person sitting right next to *you!*

MAURICE KITCHEN'S

DARK LEGENDS IN BLOOD

The Re-Mix

(A MURDER MYSTERY & MUSICAL COMEDY REVUE)

Written by Maurice Kitchen & Leonard Reed

Musical Director - T.C. Campbell

FEATURING

JESSIE BOLERO, MICHOLE BRIANA WHITE, CHERYL CARTER, LAWRENCE HILL, DARRYL ALAN REED, LES LANNOM, BOBBY MCGEE, PAM TROTTER & KRISTINE WALLACE

ALSO FEATURING KAREN MCDONALD'S NEW AGE DANCE WORKSHOP

SATURDAY, OCTOBER 22nd - 8:00 PM & SUNDAY THE 23rd, 2005, 6:00 pm

Redondo Beach Performing Arts Center

1935 Manhattan Beach Blvd

Redondo Beach, CA 90278

"...I DON'T KNOW WHEN I HAD THIS MUCH FUN WITH MY CLOTHES ON."

FOUL PLAY IS THE ORDER OF THE DAY AS THE AUDIENCE IS INVITED TO HELP UNRAVEL THIS MELLOW-DRAMATIC EVENING OF MUSIC, MURDER MAYHEM AND FUN.

DARK LEGENDS IN

BLOOD

Winner: Best Director & Musical Director
Nominated: Best Ensemble and Choreography
NAACP Theater Award 2004

Join us for a fabulous fundraiser / Theater Party
The laughter is on us. Tickets available at
Inglewood Tickets (310) 671-6400
$42.50 and $47.50 or log on to
www.darklegendsinblood.com

PLACE
STAMP
HERE

Daily Discovery - Don't Whistle Woman (Don't Crow Hen) by Jess Bolero. Rare practically unkown Funk on the Jackson label that says it's from New York but it sounds a lot more like a something from the the deep south. The flip side is a killer deep soul side. The shouting voice that Jess brings to this record sounds like a voice on the brink of breaking and he makes you feel his pain. He is pouring out of emotions like most of us only wish we had the guts too. If someone was to ask me what is Soul, it is this, pure raw emotion with no fear of who is listening.

I spoke to Jesse Bolero recently and he gave me a little more information about the the record. Robert Banks on piano, Bernard Purdie was on drums and Donny Stokes on guitar & bass, Buddy Lucas was on harmonica & sax, Jess Levy on cello and The Rose on vocals.

The producers (Rose McCoy) of "Don't Whistle Woman" wanted to promote Jesse as the black Mick Jagger. The idea was shopped to Motown producers, and after hearing his record they told Jesse that he was "too soulful". I had to laugh when Jesse told me this story, because that is what drew me to the song in the first place. Even though he doesn't think about what could have been, I wonder what his life would have been like to become a part of the Motown machine. The world will never know. Today Jesse is full of life and is still sharp, and a true showman. He is constantly thinking of new ways to reinvent himself. I am blessed to call Mr. Bolero a friend.

SOUL SOUNDS

IC MAKERS by ERNIE SHARP

RS: "THE CAB
HOW AT THE
RILL . . . It is
time at the
LL with "THE
AY SHOW" now
eatured will be
tile and talented
S CALLOWAY
nny laughmaker
. WATSON. It is
arance at the
atop Rockefeller
Calloway, the
-actor-author-
ctor, as well as
vin C.
de his new York
in "Conie's Hot

Music PULSE

By FRANK MILTON McCOY, Ph.D
Sentinel Music Critic

Cab Calloway Captivates Hollywood Bowl Audience

Appearing in a tailored white suit, the 84-year-old Calloway received a standing ovation when he made his entry on the stage, and the screams, shouts, and yells were deafening. Calloway had his audience mesmerized from his first musical note until he offered his final song. "Good Time Charlie's Got The Blues" was very well received and his voice was in good form. He had good sustaining tones, good diction, and the song was interspersed with a whistling effect.

Look-alike Jess Bolero, who portrayed Calloway in the recent local production, "Voices," accompanied me to the concert. He has perfected the persona of Calloway so closely that many persons take a second look when observing him. Calloway met Bolero backstage and he was impressed.

The "King of Hi-DE-Ho" has been in show business for over 60 years and has appeared as a bandleader, singer, and dancer in numerous Broadway shows and in films.

'VOICES' HELD OVER — Featured entertainer Jess Bolero cuts up as Cab Calloway in the hit musical sensation "Voices." An emotion-

My Name's Jesse (Not Jesse James)

Crazy World (Voices from the Past)

Pearl Bailey, Peter Lorre, Flip Wilson, Sarah Vaughan, James Brown, Jimmy Durante, Paul Robeson, Jimmy Cagney, Carol Channing, Aretha Franklin, The Kingfish, Darth Vader, Tiny Tim, Louis Armstrong, and Reverend C. L. Franklin.

The Good COUNT

MA·D
COUNT

photo's by
CHARLES
ADAMS
Mad Count will zap you with
"CRAZY
WORLD"
Photo by
CHARLES
ADAMS
Each night THE MAD COUNT uses his Time Machine to travel into FUTURE TIME! But Why? To do battle against "The Crazies," who try to warp & Destroy FUTURE TIME! Note his Radioactive eyes, throat & hair! Wild and weird man! A new hero is born!

FUTURA RECORDS
hollywood
From out of THE FUTURE comes His Excellency
"THE MAD COUNT BOLERO!"
(Theatric Sensation)
photo by
CHARLES
ADAMS
to bring you
THE GREAT SECRET,
the funniest & wildest
REVELATION OF THE CENTURY!
(in 16 different voices!)*
CRAZY WORLD! (side 1)
(we mean insane!)
plus
MY NAME'S JESSE! (side 2)
(Not Jesse James)
Collector's Edition
Says The Mad Count: "My secret purpose is to rock this world! Besides a Crusade against World Sta, we need a Crusade against WORLD INSANITY, a world gone mad! So here I am, to lead the way, you lucky people!
But beware! If anyone dares to disagree, I challenge him to a Radio-Active Duel, in FUTURE TIME! I have spoken!"

Gertrude Gipson's CANDID COMMENTS

the voice ...
lady of songville...Jess Bolero, actor/impressionist and restauranteur, has created a secret recipe with turkey..high protein/low calories and I am a living witness, his "turkey chili" is absolutely delicious..his grand opening of

H.B. BARNUM, *multi-talented arranger, conductor, composer, producer and director.*

Los Angeles Herald-Examiner, Friday, October 4, 1974 B-5

STAGE REVIEW

Marc Alaimo and Joyce Verdon star in the MET production of Lillian Hellman's 'The Little Foxes.'

some residual humor in Lillian Hellman's microcosmic, greedy family that deepens characterization. And those characters, slowly defining their depths and superficialities, remain the play's strength.

Surprisingly, the only source of dismay is the play's structure and tone, especially the last act. And that's where "The Little Foxes" seems to me inferior to MET's Inge repertoire. Hellman's plots and speeches grow mechanical, stagy, predictable. I would gladly have traded their slickness for Inge's self-tortured, often inarticulate folk. I would have traded irony for clumsy imperfection. In short, I think Inge holds up better than Hellman.

This objection is irrelevant to what Megaw, a lineal descendant of the acclaimed Northridge Theater Guild, has accomplished. Nancy Loomis and J. H. Richardson, heirs to the Giddens-Hubbard fortunes, never falter — she fresh-faced, emotionally and morally perceptive — he one of those dangerous, heavy-chinned young rich boys F. Scott Fitzgerald worried about. In the central role of Regina Giddens, flame-haired Joyce Verdon is a fine, haughty shrew, perhaps too invulnerable.

The rest are more than competent. It's not Marc Alaimo's fault he has to play a silent movie-styled heart attack. And the antic butlering of Jess Bolero, somewhere between Stepin Fetchit and Cab Calloway, may be just right after all. It's a beautifully orchestrated production.

"The Little Foxes," due for further L.A. revivals, will not get a better one, and who knows? Fridays and Saturdays 8:30, Sundays 7:30 through Oct. 26.

— JIM MOORE

NEPHEW
MINOR

LADY Bee
Jess

Jess
MANNY DAY-Bolero

About the Author

BOLERO

Jesse – The pioneer of Turkey Burgers: Bolero's no red meat restaurant in Los Angeles, quite different from the usual way people in show business change their names, Jesse, changed his by the blessing of the United States government. Christened Jesse Wilman Boler, Jr., the United States Social Security Administration made an error when they created Jesse's social security account and card by adding an "o" to the end of his given name, forever changing it from Boler to Bolero.

Daily Discovery - Don't Whistle Woman (Don't Crow Hen) by Jess Bolero. Rare practically unknown Funk on the Jackson label that says it's from New York but it sounds a lot more like a something from the deep south. The flip side is a killer deep soul side. The shouting voice that Jess brings to this record sounds like a voice on the brink of breaking and he makes you feel his pain. He is pouring out of emotions like most of us only wish we had the guts too. If someone was to ask me what is Soul, it is this, pure raw emotion with no fear of who is listening.

I spoke to Jesse Bolero recently and he gave me a little more information about the record. Robert Banks on piano, Bernard Purdie was on drums and Donny Stokes on guitar & bass, Buddy Lucas was on harmonica & sax, Jess Levy on cello and The Rose on vocals.

The producers (Rose McCoy) of "Don't Whistle Woman" wanted to promote Jesse as the black Mick Jagger. The idea was shopped to Motown producers, and after hearing his record they told Jesse that he was "too soulful". I had to laugh when Jesse told me this story, because that is what drew me to the song in the first place. Even though he doesn't think about what could have been, I wonder what his life would have been like to become a part of the Motown machine. The world will never know. Today Jesse is full of life and is still sharp, and a true showman. He is constantly thinking of new ways to reinvent himself. I am blessed to call Mr. Bolero a friend.

Jesse Bolero has served as a Senior Companions Worker for the Catholic Charities, VFW, and for both Mayors Oscar and Carolyn Goodman of Las Vegas, Nevada and for every Governor of the state of Nevada for the past 21 years. Jesse volunteers most of his time. He was also called Father Teressa. Among his achievements in show business, Jesse worked with the Blues Brothers and appeared as the legendary Cab Calloway. Jesse also served as entertainer for HUD, and the Las Vegas Housing Authority. Jesse eventually landed his first job at the Dunes Hotel appearing as Cab Calloway until the hotel was imploded.

One of his greatest highlights in his career is when he sub for actress Halle Berry for the smart Children's Award at Paramount Studios along with the Rev. Fred and Dr. Betty Price of Crenshaw Christian Center in Los Angeles, California and one of the stars of hundreds for the Los Angeles, California Central Ave Experience at Paramount Studios.

CPSIA information can be obtained
at www.ICGtesting.com
Printed in the USA
FSHW010322020620
70617FS

9 781644 629253